Merry Christmas!
Eric?

Love Mom + Dad

SNOW COUNTRY

James Skofield

PICTURES BY

Laura Jean Allen

Harper & Row, Publishers

Snow Country
Text copyright © 1983 by James Skofield
Illustrations copyright © 1983 by Laur Jean Allen

Library of Congress Cataloging in Publication Data
Skofield, James.
  Snow country.

  "A Charlotte Zolotow book."
  Summary: Two children and their grandparents wake
to a snowy day on a farm.
  [1. Snow—Fiction. 2. Farm life—Fiction
3. Grandparents—Fiction] I. Allen, Laura Jean, ill.
II. Title.
PZ7.S62835Sn 1983   [E]   82-48856
ISBN 0-06-025784-9
ISBN 0-06-025787-3 (lib. bdg.)

First Edition
1 2 3 4 5 6 7 8 9 10

For the Hubbard boys:

Oliver
Austin
Leslie and
Donald

All afternoon, the sky hangs dull and grey.
The fields and trees stand bare;
the leaves are brown.
The autumn geese are flying high and fast.
Old Woman hears that distant, urgent music;
she stops to watch the ragged lines trail south.

At supper, she warms cocoa for her grandchildren
and for her Old Man sitting by the stove.
"The geese have gone," she says; "snow comes tonight."

"How do you know?" ask Sister and Small Brother.
"She feels it in her bones," laughs out Old Man.
"It's in the wind," she smiles. "Now, bed."

With nightfall, falls the snow...
so soft, at first,

it sifts like whispers through the frozen trees...
and then, so fast,
the hollows of the hills soon fill with snow.

9

Next morning, in the silent house,
Old Woman wakes Old Man to dreams of white:
Wake up!
      There is a far and thunderous quiet!

Old Man wakes Sister
to the winter light:

Wake up!
Each fence post wears a cap of white!

And Sister wakes Small Brother
with his head beneath the covers:
O wake up!
     See the red hens in the yard!

Snow in the fields;
snowdrifts by the barn.
Snow on the town
and on the sleeping river.
Snow in the apple garth, where wise, black trees
thrust forth white blossoms to the winter air.

16

Small Brother stands
and watches from the window
while red-cheeked Sister
trudges for the mail.
Old Man does dishes.
Old Woman walks;
wrapped in winter clothes,
out to the snowy barn to do her chores.

Snow for the mare, whose breath becomes a cloud,
and for her wide-eyed yearling, shy and wild.
Snow on the meadow, where the brittle weeds
look like ink strokes upon a clean, white page.

Snow for the barn cats,
stalking down the lane.
Snow for the patient cows
inside their stalls.
Snow for Old Woman,
pitching down the hay.

Snow for Old Man,
whittling by the stove.
Snow-glare at noon
beneath a snowy sun.
Wind-brightened faces
over bowls of soup.

Snow all afternoon
for making angels.
Snowball fights, snowshoes,
snowmen on the hill.
Snow showers down
from fir trees in the woods.

Deep-blue snowshadows
when the sun sinks low.
Snowy folk stamping home
to stow their sleds.

"Snow," sings the fiddle
when the dinner's done.
"Snow," laughs the fire,
snapping, scattering sparks.
"Snow," sighs the kettle,
steaming on the hob.

"Snow," whirrs the clock,
and strikes the bedtime hour.
"Snow," yawns the sleepy family
on the stair.

Outside,
a snow moon
floods the land in light.

Silent, the fox,
who stalks the snowshoe hare.
Silent, the owl,
who floats above the hill.
Silent, the snow geese,
winging past the moon.

Inside,
Old Woman sleeps;
she dreams of foals,
while Old Man dreams
of icicles and stars.

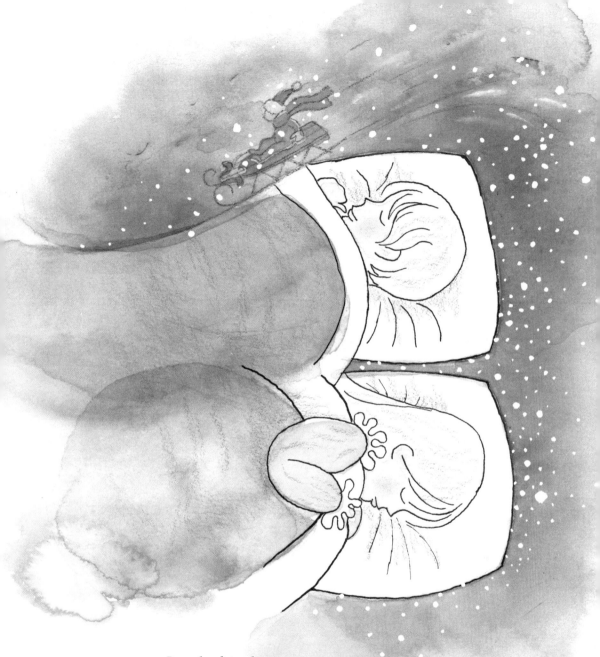

Inside *his* dream,
Small Brother slides and slides.
His sister snores;
she only dreams of white.

Sleep, snow country,
sleep to wake!
Tomorrow holds
more dreams....